W9-AWZ-614

Messy Games

"Grab a potato sack and jump in!" a teenage girl wearing a carnival cap said. She pointed to a stack of sacks.

Nancy, Bess, and George each grabbed a sack and hopped in. Twelve other kids did the same.

But as they hopped to the starting line, George slowed down. "What's that crunching noise?" she asked.

"And why do my feet feel so wet?" Bess asked.

Nancy's feet felt wet, too. And the bottom of her sack felt kind of crunchy.

"Uh-oh," Nancy said. She stepped out of her sack. Her blue sneakers were covered with sticky yellow stuff. Nancy peeked inside her sack.

"Oh, no!" she cried. "My sack is filled with raw eggs!"

The Nancy Drew Notebooks

Available from Simon & Schuster

THE
NANCY DREW
NOTEBOOKS®

#48

The Crazy Carnival Case

CAROLYN KEENE
ILLUSTRATED BY JAN NAIMO JONES

Aladdin Paperbacks
New York   London   Toronto   Sydney   Singapore

If you purchased this book without a cover, you should be aware that this book is stolen property. It was reported as "unsold and destroyed" to the publisher and neither the author nor the publisher has received any payment for this "stripped book."

This book is a work of fiction. Any references to historical events, real people, or real locales are used fictitiously. Other names, characters, places, and incidents are the product of the author's imagination, and any resemblance to actual events or locales or persons, living or dead, is entirely coincidental.

First Aladdin Paperbacks edition June 2002

Copyright © 2002 by Simon & Schuster, Inc.

ALADDIN PAPERBACKS
An imprint of Simon & Schuster
Children's Publishing Division
1230 Avenue of the Americas
New York, NY 10020

All rights reserved, including the right of reproduction in whole or in part in any form.

The text of this book was set in Excelsior.

Printed in the United States of America
10 9 8 7 6 5 4 3 2 1

Library of Congress Control Number: 2001097938

NANCY DREW and THE NANCY DREW NOTEBOOKS
are registered trademarks of Simon & Schuster, Inc.

ISBN 0-7434-3747-0

1

Coconut Scream Pie

Bess!" eight-year-old Nancy Drew said to her best friend. "The pie-eating contest hasn't started yet!"

"I know," Bess Marvin said. She licked whipped cream off her thumb. "But practice makes perfect. This is just a sample."

George Fayne, Nancy's other best friend, leaned her elbows on the long picnic table inside the tent where the contest was about to take place. George's real name was Georgia. "When *aren't* you practicing, Bess?" she asked.

Nancy smiled. It was a sunny Monday in late June. School was out for the summer. It was also the first day of the River Heights Carnival. The girls were excited to be there.

The carnival was held every year behind Riverbank Middle School. For a whole week people came to enjoy the games, contests, and yummy food. There was even a piano-playing chicken named Henrietta Von Peck.

The girls had permission to go to the carnival every day. But this year would be extra-special. The girls' favorite singer, Isabelle Santoro, would be singing at the carnival on Thursday.

Isabelle was fifteen years old and lived in River Heights. She had sung on the TV show *Mr. Lizard's Funhouse* twice and even had her own song on the radio.

"Look!" Bess said, pointing. "That must be first prize!"

Nancy looked to see where Bess was pointing. A giant stuffed panda stood near the opening of the pie-eating tent.

"I just remembered something," George said. "Isabelle once told Mr. Lizard that she collects pandas."

"I know!" Nancy said. "If one of us wins

the pie-eating contest, let's give the panda to Isabelle."

The three friends gave one another high-fives. Then a tall girl with short brown hair walked into the tent.

"Oh, no!" Bess wailed. She tugged at her blond ponytail. "It's Chloe Mondesky!"

"You mean *Cruncher* Mondesky." George groaned. "We don't have a chance."

Nancy's heart sank. Cruncher was eight years old and went to school in the next town. She had been the pie-eating champ for two years in a row.

Cruncher grinned as she ripped open a jumbo chocolate and caramel candy bar.

"Look!" Nancy whispered. "Cruncher is eating a candy bar. Maybe she's spoiling her appetite."

"Or just warming up," George said. Her dark curls bounced as she shook her head. "Cruncher eats everything in sight."

"Not everything," Bess said in a whisper. "Last year I heard Cruncher tell someone that she hates coconuts."

"Big deal," Nancy said. "The pies in the

contest are banana cream. They are every year."

Cruncher took a seat at the table. There were six other tables in the tent. All of them were filled with hungry kids.

"Excuse me," a girl's voice broke in. "Is this the place for the pig-out contest?"

Nancy groaned. She'd know that voice anywhere. It was Brenda Carlton.

Brenda was in the girls' third-grade class at Carl Sandburg Elementary School. She was very nosy and very snooty.

"It's the *pie-eating* contest," Nancy corrected. "Did you enter, too, Brenda?"

Brenda took a seat at Nancy's table. "No way," she said. "I'm writing about the carnival for my newspaper, the *Carlton News*. It comes out once a week, you know."

"And you remind us about it every single day," George complained.

"Why don't you write about Isabelle?" Bess suggested. "She rocks!"

"She sings like a parrot with crackers in her mouth," Brenda said.

"Nuh-uh!" Bess snapped.

"Uh-huh!" Brenda snapped back.

4

"Welcome, kids!" a man wearing a baker's hat interrupted.

"It's Simon the Pieman!" Nancy said.

Simon's booth at the carnival looked like a fairy-tale cottage. He sold the yummiest mini-pies. They had names like Little Boy Blueberry and Mother Gooseberry.

Even Simon's kids—triplets—got into the act. Every summer Nicky, Vicky, and Ricky dressed up as the Three Little Pigs. Their job was to walk around the carnival reminding everyone to try Simon's pies.

"Are you kids ready to dig into my pies?" Simon called out. He walked around the tent, putting a pie in front of each kid.

"Not yet," Bess said. She neatly laid a napkin over her crisp white pants. "Don't you want a napkin, George?"

"What for?" George asked. She rolled up the sleeves of her T-shirt.

"What will you do if you get whipped cream all over you?" Bess asked.

George shrugged. "Lick it off!"

Nancy giggled. She still couldn't believe Bess and George were cousins. They were so different.

"Okay—on your mark!" Simon began to shout. "Get set. And go!"

Nancy brushed back her reddish blond hair and grabbed her pie. She was about to lean over when she heard a loud splat.

Glancing to the side, Nancy saw Cruncher. Her whole face was buried in her pie.

Then Cruncher jerked her face up. "Yuck! These pies aren't banana cream. They're . . . they're coconut!"

"Sorry," Simon said. "But Shirley Vega wanted a new flavor this year. And she's the director of the carnival."

"You mean she wanted a new champ!" Cruncher growled. "I wouldn't eat coconuts if I were stranded on a desert island!"

Cruncher grabbed a wad of napkins and wiped cream off her face. Then she ripped into another candy bar and stormed out.

"What a story!" Brenda exclaimed. She began writing as she left the tent. "Champ loses title but not her appetite!"

Nancy shook her head. Couldn't Brenda write about something nice for a change?

The contest went on without Cruncher. Nancy, Bess, and George ate as fast as they could. But in the end, the winner was a nine-year-old boy named Tyrone.

"Oh, well." Nancy sighed as Tyrone took the panda. "So I won't be the pie-eating champ this year."

"But you'll always be the school's best detective," Bess pointed out.

Nancy smiled. She did love solving mysteries more than anything. She even had a blue detective notebook where she wrote down all her suspects and clues.

The girls left the pie-eating tent and walked through the carnival.

Nancy hardly recognized the middle school. Game booths and food stands were lined up next to the building. On the soccer field stood a kiddy Ferris wheel, a bouncy castle, and a twenty-five-foot caterpillar tunnel.

Nancy could hear croaking sounds coming from the frog-jumping contest on the basketball court.

"We have a whole hour before Bess's mom picks us up," Nancy said, glancing at her watch. "Why don't we play some — "

"*Bluuuuurp!*"

Nancy didn't finish her sentence. Something cold and wet landed on her right shoulder. She looked over and screamed.

Sitting on her shoulder was a big, slimy bullfrog!

2
Sack Attack!

Eww!" Nancy cried. She wiggled her shoulder, and the bullfrog hopped off.

"Give me Frogzilla!" a boy's voice demanded. "Give him to me now!"

Nancy saw Orson Wong running toward them. Orson was in the girls' class. He was nice, but he could be a pest sometimes.

"It's not fair!" Orson said. He reached down and grabbed the croaking frog by its middle. "It's unjust!"

Orson was wearing a white T-shirt with the words FROGZILLA RULES printed on it. Strapped over his shoulder was a plastic carrying case with tiny holes.

"Frogzilla was supposed to be in the frog-jumping contest," Orson said. "But he was disqualified."

"What does that mean?" Bess asked.

"It means Frogzilla isn't allowed to jump," Orson said. "The director said I gave him a push."

"Did you?" Nancy asked.

"No way!" Orson said. He shrugged. "It was a high-five. For good luck."

"*Bluuuurp!*" Frogzilla croaked.

Nancy could see Brenda standing nearby. Her head was tilted as if she was listening to every word.

"I don't get it," Orson went on. "The rules say we can walk next to our frogs. We can blow on them. Why can't we give them a high-five?"

"Rules are rules," Nancy said.

"Rules, shmules!" Orson said. "Frogzilla trained for this race for weeks. I even put him on a special diet!"

Orson pulled a jar of giant black horse-flies from his pants pocket.

"Ewww!" Bess cried.

"I caught these beauties myself," Orson

said proudly. "Premium Grade-A pests!"

"It takes one to know one," George whispered to Nancy.

"I heard that!" Orson snapped. He shoved the jar back in his pocket. Then he placed Frogzilla into his carrying case.

"We'll show this stupid carnival," Orson muttered. "Right, Frogzilla?"

"Bluuurp!" Frogzilla croaked.

Orson marched away with Frogzilla swinging from his shoulder.

"What did Orson mean by that?" Bess asked. "That they'll show the carnival?"

"It's just pest talk," George said.

Brenda ran over, waving her reporter pad. "Check out this headline," she said, "'Frog contestant hopping mad!'"

"Why don't you write about something nice?" Nancy asked. "Like the new Ferris wheel at the carnival."

"Did it get stuck yet?" Brenda asked, her eyes shining. "Or make anyone sick?"

"No," Nancy said.

"Then what good is it?" Brenda said. She flipped her hair over her shoulder and walked to the honey-roasted peanut stand.

"Come on." Nancy sighed. "Let's forget about Brenda and play some games."

First the girls played the beanbag toss, then the color wheel, and finally the giant ring toss.

Nancy flung the plastic ring. She held her breath as it landed on top of the old-fashioned milk bottle. But instead of circling it, it fell right off.

"Rats!" Nancy said. She pointed to the shelf filled with toys. "I wanted to win that stuffed panda for Isabelle."

"We all did," Bess said.

"There's still the big potato sack race tomorrow," George said. "I'll bet there'll be more pandas there."

"Yes!" Nancy cheered under her breath. The potato sack race was her favorite contest of all.

The girls joined arms and skipped toward the balloon gate to meet Mrs. Marvin. Nancy heard some giggling.

She turned and saw the triplets, Nicky, Vicky, and Ricky. They were dressed in their usual Three Little Pigs costumes.

The costumes looked like fuzzy pink

pajamas. Written on the back of each was
PIG OUT AT SIMON THE PIEMAN'S.

The costumes covered the triplets from
head to toe, but their hands were free. Free
enough to hold ice cream cones, bags of
nuts, and cotton candy.

"Nicky! Vicky! Ricky!" Nancy called.

The Three Little Pigs spun around. They
stared out of the eyeholes in their hood-
masks.

"Hi!" Nancy said, waving.

The triplets waved their cones and cotton
candy. Then they scurried away.

"Where are they going?" Nancy asked.

"Maybe to hog some more food." Bess
giggled.

"Cute!" George said.

Mrs. Marvin picked the girls up in her
red minivan. Nancy was the first to be
driven home.

When Nancy ran into the kitchen Hannah
Gruen was placing fresh-baked cookies
on a plate. Hannah had been the Drews'
housekeeper since Nancy was only three
years old.

"Hannah, do we have any potato sacks?"

Nancy asked. "I want to practice for the potato sack race tomorrow."

"No," Hannah said with a smile. "But we've got plenty of pillowcases."

"Hannah, you're a genius!" Nancy said. She grabbed a cookie. "And a pretty amazing cook, too. But I think I'll save this for later."

Upstairs in her room Nancy hopped back and forth inside a flowered pillowcase. Her Labrador puppy, Chocolate Chip, wagged her tail and chased her.

Nancy felt the pillowcase tangle around her legs. She fell down on the rug. Chip began licking her face.

"Great!" Nancy giggled. "It's a good thing I'm not a potato. Or I'd be mashed!"

At eleven the next morning Hannah drove the girls to the carnival. She promised to pick them up at two o'clock sharp.

The girls got their carnival passbooks stamped with the date. Then they ran through the balloon gate.

"Look!" Bess cried, pointing. "It's Isabelle Santoro!"

Nancy's heart flipped when she saw Isabelle Santoro standing a few feet away.

But as they ran closer, Nancy could see it wasn't Isabelle at all.

"It's a cardboard cut-out," Nancy said, tapping Isabelle's face. "But don't worry. We'll see the real Isabelle soon."

An announcement came over the loudspeaker. The potato sack race would begin in ten minutes on the soccer field.

"Wait for meeee!" Brenda called as she ran through the balloon gate.

"Are you in the potato sack race, too, Brenda?" Nancy asked.

"And crawl into a dusty old bag?" Brenda scoffed. "I'm here in case something exciting happens at the race."

"She means in case someone slips and falls," George whispered to Nancy.

"I heard that!" Brenda snapped.

The girls ran to the soccer field.

"Hi, I'm Nina," a teenage girl wearing a carnival cap said with a smile. "Grab a potato sack and jump in!"

She pointed to a stack of sacks. Some of them were thick and brown. Others had been made from brightly colored sheets and blankets.

Down the field was a red ribbon finish line. Near it were a few stuffed animals.

One was a panda!

The girls each grabbed a sack and hopped in. Twelve other kids did the same.

But as they hopped to the starting line, George slowed down. "What's that crunching noise?" she asked.

"And why do my feet feel so wet?" Bess asked.

Nancy's feet felt wet, too. And the bottom of her sack felt kind of crunchy.

"Uh-oh," Nancy said. She stepped out of her sack. Her blue sneakers were covered with sticky yellow stuff.

Nancy peeked inside her sack.

"Oh, no!" she cried. "My sack is filled with raw eggs!"

3
Carnival Creep

My sack is filled with eggs, too!" George cried. She shook a dripping foot. "Look at my gross sneakers!"

Bess was wearing sandals. "Look at my gross toes!" she wailed.

Other kids stepped out of their sacks. Their feet were messy, too.

While the kids tried to clean their sneakers a woman with bright red hair hurried over. She was carrying a clipboard and wearing a yellow carnival cap.

"It's Shirley Vega," Bess whispered. "The director of the carnival."

"What's this about eggs in the potato sacks?" Shirley demanded.

Nancy could see Brenda inching her way over with her reporter pad.

"I don't know how it happened, Shirley," Nina said. "I brought the potato sacks out before the carnival opened. They were perfectly clean then."

"It's not your fault, Nina," Shirley said. She narrowed her eyes. "Someone is making trouble at the carnival. This isn't the first thing to happen."

"Does this mean there won't be a potato sack race?" a girl asked.

"Not if I can help it!" Shirley said. She turned to Nina. "There are more sacks inside the school. Let's get them."

Shirley and Nina went inside the school. Nancy and her friends found a water hose to wash off their icky feet.

"That's it!" Brenda called as she ran over. "The perfect story for my paper. 'Trouble at the River Heights Carnival!'"

"Don't, Brenda," Nancy warned. "Then nobody will come to the carnival."

"And Isabelle might not come either," Bess said.

"So what?" Brenda said. "I told you she sings like a parrot."

George pointed the water hose at Brenda, but Nancy grabbed her arm.

"And speaking of Isabelle," Brenda said. "Maybe I'll give her a copy of my newspaper. I do know where she lives."

"You wouldn't!" Nancy said.

Brenda began to walk away. "A good reporter always tells the truth."

"Wait!" Bess called out. "If Nancy finds the troublemaker will you forget about the article?"

"Bess!" Nancy said. "I didn't come to the carnival to solve a mystery."

"But you did bring your detective notebook, didn't you?" Bess asked.

"Yes . . . but," Nancy said slowly. She carried her notebook wherever she went.

"Then you came to solve a mystery!" Bess said cheerily. She turned to Brenda. "Well? Is it a deal or not?"

"I guess," Brenda said. She pointed a finger

at Nancy. "But you have to solve your case by Wednesday."

"That's tomorrow!" Nancy complained.

"I know," Brenda said. "I want to finish my article tomorrow night. That way I can deliver my papers Thursday morning."

Nancy frowned. Thursday was the day Isabelle was supposed to sing. She had to do something!

"Okay," Nancy told Brenda. "But only if you agree to one more thing."

"What?" Brenda asked.

"That if I find the troublemaker, you'll write something *nice*," Nancy said.

"Nice?" Brenda choked. "You mean, like the Ferris wheel? The bunnies in the petting zoo? The new taffy flavor?"

Nancy nodded. "Do we have a deal?"

"Yes, we have a deal," Brenda said. "But only because I don't think you'll do it."

Nancy ignored what Brenda had said. She held out her hand to shake, but Brenda jumped back.

"Yuck—eggy!" Brenda cried. Then she turned on her heel and walked away.

"Leave it to Miss Snooty Pants to spoil the carnival," Bess said.

"Brenda's not spoiling it," Nancy said. "The carnival creep is."

"Let's go back," George said. "I see Nina coming with the clean sacks."

The race began again, but Nancy, Bess, and George lost to a tall girl with long legs.

"Another panda down the drain." George sighed.

Nancy was sad that she didn't win, but she was excited to start her new case.

As she and her friends walked back toward the school building they saw Chloe Mondesky. She was carrying a bag of honey-roasted peanuts.

"Hi, Cruncher," the girls said.

"Mmph," Cruncher said through a mouthful of peanuts.

"Check it out," George whispered as Cruncher walked away. "She's wearing a blue ribbon on her shirt."

"It's probably from last year," Nancy decided. "So she can remind everyone that she was once the pie-eating champ."

The girls sat down on a wooden bench in

front of the beanbag toss.

Nancy pulled her blue detective notebook from the pocket of her shorts. She opened to a clean page and wrote, "The Case of the Carnival Creep."

"Creep is right," George said. "Who would want to make trouble at a carnival?"

"It can't be Jason, David, and Mike this time," Nancy said.

Jason Hutchings, David Berger, and Mike Minelli were the biggest troublemakers in the girls' class. But Nancy hadn't seen them at the carnival yet.

"What about Brenda?" Bess asked. "Maybe she's causing trouble so she can write about it for her newspaper."

Nancy shook her head. "Brenda came into the carnival the same time we did."

"And she would never get her hands messy with gross eggs," George added.

Nancy thought hard.

"Maybe it's someone who's mad at the carnival," she said. "Like Cruncher. She was really mad about those coconut pies."

"Or Orson," George added. "He was steaming when Frogzilla was disqualified."

Nancy wrote "Cruncher" and "Orson" in her notebook. She was happy to have two suspects. But she still needed clues.

The girls ran back to the soccer field. Nancy searched the area where the potato sacks had been stacked. She found an empty peanut bag and a paper cone from a slushy.

"None of the contestants were eating," Nancy said. "So these might have belonged to the carnival creep."

Nancy slipped the evidence between the pages of her notebook. But as the girls walked back to the booths she was puzzled.

"The wrappers came from the carnival," Nancy said. "But where did all those raw eggs come from?"

Just then a loud cheer filled the air. Nancy turned and saw a crowd standing in front of a small stage. On the stage was a chicken pecking at a toy piano.

"It's Henrietta!" George cried.

Nancy's eyes opened wide. "Chickens lay eggs," she said. "Maybe the raw eggs came from Henrietta Von Peck!"

Nancy and her friends ran closer to the

stage. They stood on their tiptoes to see over the crowd. Standing next to the stage was a short bald man. He was wearing a yellow suit and a red bowtie—chicken colors.

"There's Henrietta's manager, Lou Fowler," Nancy pointed out. "He's here with Henrietta every year."

A few feet away from the stage was a striped tent. Above the tent opening was a gold star with the initials *HVP.*

"That's got to be Henrietta's tent," Nancy said. "Let's check it out."

The girls squeezed through the crowd. While Henrietta pecked out "Twinkle, Twinkle, Little Star," they slipped into the tent.

The first things Nancy saw were white feathers scattered on the ground.

"Are those Henrietta's?" Bess asked.

"Probably," George said. "Unless she and Lou had a pillow fight."

The girls searched the tent. Nancy found a wire cage, a hot plate, frying pan, and finally—a bucket of eggs.

"Wait!" Nancy said. "The eggshells in the

sacks were white. Those eggs are brown."

"Buck! Buck! Buck!"

Nancy spun around. A ruffled white chicken was flapping into the tent.

It was Henrietta. And she looked mad!

4
What's the Buzz?

Go away!" Nancy whispered. She froze as Henrietta began pecking at her sneakers.

"Who's in there?" a gruff voice demanded.

"Nobody here but us chickens!" George called back.

The tent door parted. Lou Fowler marched in. "Aha!" he declared. "I knew somebody was in here."

"How did you know?" Nancy asked.

"A little birdy told me so!" Lou said, his bowtie bobbing. "Henrietta has an ear for music—and for trouble."

"We weren't making trouble, Mr. Fowler,"

Nancy said. "We were just looking for Henrietta's eggs."

"*Buck!*" Henrietta clucked.

"Her eggs?" Lou cried. He glared at Nancy. "What are you—some kind of fox?"

"No!" Nancy said. She didn't want to tell Lou everything. Not until she was sure the eggs came from Henrietta.

"We just heard that Henrietta lays such fresh eggs," George said.

Lou smiled. He looked proud.

"See for yourself," Lou said. He picked up an egg and the frying pan. "How do you like 'em—scrambled or over easy?"

"*Buuuuck!*" Henrietta clucked.

Nancy stepped back. She wanted to investigate the eggs, not eat them.

"No thanks," Nancy said. "But please tell us why the eggs are so brown."

"It's because Henrietta is a Rhode Island Red chicken," Lou said. "They all lay brown eggs. But don't ask me why."

Nancy was disappointed. Henrietta's eggs weren't the ones they were looking for.

"Thanks, Mr. Fowler," Nancy said. "But I do have one more question."

"What?" Lou asked.

"How does Henrietta know how to play all those songs?" Nancy asked.

"How else?" Lou asked. His eyes twinkled. "She wings it!"

The girls said goodbye to Henrietta. Then they left her tent.

"If those chickens lay brown eggs," Bess said, "why don't they call them Rhode Island Browns?"

"Who knows?" Nancy said. "But I do know one thing. The eggs in the sacks were not Henrietta's."

"Then where did those eggs come from?" George asked. "It's not like they sell cartons of raw eggs at the carnival."

"The troublemaker must have brought the eggs to the carnival," Nancy decided.

Nancy stopped to write her thoughts inside her notebook.

"Maybe the carnival creep won't make any more trouble," Bess said. "Maybe he or she gave up after the potato sacks."

"I hope so," Nancy said. As she shut her notebook she saw Brenda waving.

"Oh, Detective Drew!" Brenda called.

"Wait until you see what I found!"

Nancy, Bess, and George followed Brenda to the cutout of Isabelle Santoro.

Nancy's mouth dropped open. A black mustache was drawn on Isabelle's cardboard face. Her eyes were marked to look as if they were crossed.

"Who did this?" Nancy demanded.

"That's your job," Brenda said with a grin. "You're the detective!"

Then Brenda took out a camera and snapped a picture of the cutout.

"What are you doing?" George asked.

"It's for my article," Brenda replied. "I thought Isabelle might want to see what she looks like with a mustache."

"That's not nice!" Nancy scolded.

"I know," Brenda said. "But I don't have to write a nice article. Yet."

Nancy felt her cheeks burn as Brenda walked away. "Let's catch that carnival creep," she said. "Once and for all!"

Nancy walked around the cutout looking for clues. She found two candy wrappers by Isabelle's cardboard feet.

"Those must be Cruncher's," George said.

"Who else eats that much candy?"

"We'll show them," a voice muttered. "We'll show them. We'll show them. . . ."

Nancy saw Orson Wong walking by. Over his shoulder was Frogzilla's carrying case. In Orson's arms were bags of candy bars, taffy, and jelly beans.

"Orson with loads of candy," Nancy whispered. "And he's a suspect, too."

"Orson!" George yelled. "Wait up!"

Orson looked over his shoulder. His mouth dropped open, and he began to run.

"Get him!" Nancy ordered.

The girls ran after Orson. They chased him around the carnival booths and the snack stands. Then they lost him.

"Look!" George said. She pointed to the ground. "A trail of jelly beans!"

The girls followed the jelly bean trail to the soccer field. They found a few more jelly beans but no Orson.

Nancy looked around and saw the caterpillar tunnel. It gave her an idea.

"Maybe he hid in there," Nancy said.

Nancy, Bess, and George had to duck a bit as they walked inside the caterpillar.

"We caught you taffy-handed, Orson!" George called out. "So give yourself up!"

The girls were halfway through the caterpillar when Nancy stopped.

"What's that buzzing noise?" Nancy asked in a hushed voice.

"What buzzing noise?" Bess asked.

Nancy saw a big fat fly land on Bess's nose. Then one on her arm. And on her forehead.

"Eeek!" Bess shrieked. Her eyes crossed as she swatted the fly from her nose.

"Attack!" George cried as flies dotted her own arms and legs.

Nancy screamed, too.

The caterpillar tunnel was filled with big, black horseflies!

5

Tattoo Clue

It's a swarm!" George cried.

Nancy gasped as a horsefly landed on her forehead. "Let's get out of here!"

Covering their faces, the girls raced through the caterpillar.

"Safe!" George gasped as they stumbled out at the other end.

When Nancy uncovered her face she saw Orson Wong. He was standing outside the caterpillar and staring at them.

"Blurrrp!" Frogzilla croaked from inside his case.

"Get away from meeee!" Orson yelled as he spun around on his heel.

The chase went on—this time all the way to the balloon gate.

"Stop, Orson!" Nancy called. "We just want to ask you some questions!"

Orson did stop. He pulled Frogzilla out and held it in front of his face.

"Back! Back!" Orson demanded. "Or you'll get warts! Giant oozy warts!"

"Bluuurp!" Frogzilla croaked.

The girls jumped back. They stayed silent as Orson ran out of the gate and into his dad's car.

"He's guilty all right!" Bess said. "Did you see the way he ran from us?"

"And all that candy?" George asked. "There were candy wrappers at the scenes of all the crimes."

Nancy pulled out her detective notebook. "And Orson did have a big jar of horseflies yesterday," she said. "Maybe he let them loose in the caterpillar."

"To make more trouble!" Bess added. Next to Orson's name Nancy wrote "candy wrappers" and "horseflies."

"What do we do now?" Bess asked.

Nancy looked at her watch. Hannah

would pick them up in a half an hour.

"We have just enough time to get rub-on tattoos," Nancy said.

"Great!" George said. "Maybe I'll get a butterfly."

"George!" Bess shuddered. "Did you have to say *fly*?"

The girls each decided to get the temporary carnival tattoo on her hand. It showed a friendly red dragon wearing a yellow River Heights Carnival cap.

When the tattoos dried, the girls ran to the balloon gate to meet Hannah.

Nancy smiled when she saw her father drive up instead.

"Hi, girls!" Mr. Drew called from the car window. "I left the office early so I could pick you up."

"Thanks, Daddy!" Nancy said.

All three girls climbed into the backseat and buckled their seat belts.

"Did you all have a good time at the carnival?" Mr. Drew asked.

"Yes," Bess said.

"And no," George added.

Nancy told her father everything—the

eggy potato sacks, the messed-up cutout, and the fly-filled caterpillar.

"If I don't solve this case in one day," Nancy said, "we'll be dancing to Henrietta Von Peck instead of Isabelle!"

"Don't worry," Mr. Drew said. "A carnival is full of surprises. You never know what you'll find."

Nancy smiled. Her father was a lawyer. He always gave good advice. But this time Nancy needed more than that.

She needed good *luck*!

"'Candy wrappers,'" Nancy read from her notebook later. "'Horseflies . . .'"

It was just before dinner. Nancy was sitting on her doorstep with her notebook on her lap. Her puppy, Chip, wagged her tail as Nancy studied her notes.

"One clue leads to Cruncher," Nancy said. "The other to Orson. But who is it?"

Chip barked. Nancy looked up. She saw three cone-shaped heads bobbing above the Drews' hedge.

"Another mystery, Detective Drew?" a voice behind the hedge asked.

Nancy frowned. She knew that voice. It belonged to Jason Hutchings.

Jason, David, and Mike ran into her yard. They were wearing their *Moleheads from Mars* costumes.

"Our spaceship has landed!" Jason announced. "Take us to your leader!"

"Or to your kitchen," Mike said. He rubbed his stomach. "We're hungry!"

Nancy rolled her eyes. *Moleheads from Mars* was the boys' favorite TV show. They loved to dress up as aliens and act silly.

"How come you weren't at the carnival yesterday or today?" Nancy asked.

"We *hate* the carnival!" David said.

"Why?" Nancy asked. She couldn't imagine anyone not liking the carnival.

"Because we wanted to be Isabelle Santoro's opening act," Jason explained.

"And do what?" Nancy asked.

"Sing the Molehead rap," Jason said. "But Shirley said only Isabelle can sing at the carnival."

"So who needs the carnival?" Mike growled. He turned to his friends. "Hit it, guys!"

Nancy wrinkled her nose as Jason, David, and Mike began to shout.

"We're Moleheads from Mars,
And we're in your face!
We won't stop invading
Till we rule Outer Space!"

Nancy gritted her teeth. For the big finish the boys blared their Mars radar blasters.

"Time out!" Nancy shouted, covering her ears. "The show is over!"

"Moleheads rule!" the boys declared. They held up three clenched fists.

That's when Nancy saw them: three rub-on carnival tattoos. The same dragon tattoos that she, Bess, and George had gotten!

"To the spaceship!" Jason declared.

Then the Moleheads from Mars marched out of Nancy's yard.

"Chip," Nancy said slowly. "If the boys weren't at the carnival, then how did they get those carnival tattoos?"

6

Creamed!

Are you sure they were carnival tattoos?" Bess asked Nancy the next day.

Nancy nodded. It was late Wednesday morning. Mr. Fayne had just dropped the girls off at the carnival.

"But we'd know if the boys were at the carnival," George told Nancy. "They're always annoying us."

"That's what makes it so strange," Nancy said.

The girls waited to get their carnival passbooks stamped. But this time Nancy was not so excited.

"It's Wednesday," Nancy said. "And we

haven't come close to solving this case."

"And we still haven't bought pies from Simon the Pieman!" Bess complained.

They were getting their passbooks stamped when Nancy saw their classmates Molly Angelo and Amara Shane. They were on their way out.

"Are you coming back later?" Nancy asked.

"No way!" Amara answered. She held up her hands. "The handles in the Big Squirt game were covered with molasses!"

"Our hands are still sticky," Molly added. "And we washed them three times!"

Nancy waved goodbye to Amara and Molly. Then she turned to Bess and George.

"Molasses on the handles," Nancy said. "Sounds like more trouble."

At that moment Shirley Vega walked by with Lou Fowler. He was carrying Henrietta.

"What do you mean Henrietta won't play the piano today?" Shirley was asking.

"I told you, Shirley," Lou said. "Henrietta's gold star is missing. Someone must have snatched it right off her tent."

"So what?" Shirley said. "Why can't she play?"

"Because that was her lucky star!" Lou wailed. "And Henrietta can't play without her lucky star!"

"Buuuck!" Henrietta clucked.

"Did you hear that?" Nancy whispered. "Someone stole Henrietta's star."

"More trouble!" Bess groaned.

Nancy pulled out her notebook. She made a list of all the things the carnival creep had used to make trouble: eggs, a black marker, horseflies, and molasses.

"Speaking of trouble," George muttered, "here comes Brenda."

"Did you hear about the sticky handles?" Brenda called as she ran over. "And Henrietta's gold star?"

"We heard." Nancy sighed.

"Am I lucky or what?" Brenda cried. "Now I have enough stuff to start writing my article!"

"Not fair, Brenda," Nancy said. "I still have today to solve the case."

"Calm down," Brenda said. "I said I'd

start writing the article. I didn't say I'd deliver the papers yet."

Nancy breathed a small sigh of relief. As long as Brenda didn't deliver the paper to Isabelle, they were safe.

"Can we please get some mini-pies?" Bess asked. "I can smell them from here."

Nancy glanced over at Simon the Pieman's booth. She saw a bunch of people waiting on line. One of them was Chloe "Cruncher" Mondesky.

Nancy watched as Cruncher stepped up to the counter. She was wearing a big red backpack, and it was wide open.

"I'm going to peek in Cruncher's backpack," Nancy told Bess and George. "I want to see if she has molasses or a lucky star."

"Cruncher is one of your suspects?" Brenda asked in an excited whisper. "Let me look in her backpack."

"Why you?" Nancy asked.

"Because that will make me an investigative reporter," Brenda declared. "Sort of like a reporter *and* a detective."

"No, Brenda," Nancy said. "Don't—"

Nancy's plea came too late. Brenda was

already sneaking up behind Cruncher.

Brenda leaned forward. Then she reached into Cruncher's backpack.

"Hey!" Cruncher spun around. The mini-pie she had just bought flew out of her hand. It landed with a splat in Brenda's surprised face.

Nancy couldn't keep from giggling. Brenda had pumpkin mush dripping from her nose and her chin.

"Nuts!" Cruncher grumbled. "I was going to eat that."

"Pa-tooey!" Brenda sputtered as she wiped cream off her mouth.

"I hope you like Peter, Peter, Pumpkin Pie," George said as she, Bess, and Nancy ran over.

Brenda wiped cream from her eyes. Then she glared at Nancy.

"That does it," Brenda said. "I'm going home to write my article—once and for all!"

"Oh no, you don't," Cruncher said. "First you're going to tell me what you were doing in my backpack."

"Ask Nancy," Brenda snapped as she huffed off. "She'll tell you."

Cruncher folded her arms. "Which one of you is Nancy?" she asked.

"Um," George gulped.

"Er," Bess squeaked.

Nancy looked up at Cruncher. She was big for an eight-year-old.

"I'm Nancy," Nancy said bravely.

"Well?" Cruncher said. "Why was that girl going through my backpack?"

Nancy had no choice. She had to get right to the point.

"I'm a detective," Nancy explained. "There's been trouble at the carnival. And some of the clues lead to . . . you."

"Me?" Cruncher snapped.

"You were mad at the carnival for using coconut cream pies," George said. "Mad enough to make trouble."

Nancy expected Cruncher to explode. Instead she smiled and shrugged.

"I *was* mad at the carnival," Cruncher said. "But not anymore."

"Why not?" Nancy asked.

Cruncher opened her jacket to show the blue ribbon pinned to her T-shirt.

"Because I'm the new chocolate pudding

eating champ!" she declared. "I won the contest yesterday!"

Nancy stared at the ribbon. It was the same blue ribbon she had seen on Cruncher the day before.

"But you still could have put eggs in the potato sacks sometime before the contest," Nancy pointed out.

"How could I?" Cruncher asked. "The pudding eating contest was the same time as the potato sack race yesterday."

To prove it, Cruncher took out the carnival schedule.

Nancy looked at Tuesday's schedule. Cruncher was right. The two contests were at the same time. But that didn't answer all of Nancy's questions.

She pulled the candy wrappers out from her detective notebook.

"Then how do you explain these?" Nancy asked Cruncher.

7

Hogs and Frogs

May I see those candy wrappers?" Cruncher asked.

After examining each wrapper Cruncher began to laugh.

"What's so funny?" George asked.

Cruncher didn't answer. She grinned and held up a green candy wrapper.

"*Coconut* Crunchy?" Cruncher said. "Would I eat a coconut candy bar? I don't think so!"

Nancy stared at the wrapper and blushed. "I guess I should have read the wrappers first," she said.

"Nobody's perfect," Cruncher said with a smile. "So, am I clean?"

"Yes," Nancy told her.

"But your friend with the pumpkin pie face sure wasn't!" Cruncher joked. She gave a little wave and walked away.

"Now we have only one suspect." Nancy sighed. She crossed Cruncher's name out of her notebook. "Orson Wong."

Nancy was about to shut her notebook when she heard snickering. She glanced up and saw the Three Little Pigs standing behind the pie booth counter. They were holding mini-pies.

"Hi!" Nancy called.

The three ducked behind the counter.

"What's with them?" Nancy asked.

"Who knows?" George said. "Maybe they're afraid of the Big Bad Wolf."

Nancy, Bess, and George walked through the carnival looking for Orson. But he was nowhere in sight.

"Maybe Orson came early this morning," George said. "Some of the trouble did happen before we got here."

"We can still question Orson tomorrow,"

Bess suggested. "After we buy some pies from Simon the Pieman."

Nancy's heart sank. The next day was Thursday. That was the day that Brenda planned to deliver the *Carlton News* — and her horrible article!

"We have to find Orson today," Nancy said. "Even if it means going to his house."

"His house?" Bess gasped. "Then we'd better bring along some pest spray."

"For the horseflies?" Nancy asked.

"No," Bess said. "For Orson!"

The girls finally bought mini-pies from Simon. Afterward Nancy wanted to question some people at the carnival — like Trish, the owner of the Big Squirt.

"Did you see anyone pour molasses on the squirt handles, Trish?" Nancy asked.

"Nope," Trish said. "I keep my eye on all the kids who play this game."

"Then did anyone have messy or sticky hands?" Nancy asked.

Trish laughed. "This is a carnival," she said. "Everyone has messy and sticky hands!"

Next Nancy wanted to question Lou Fowler, but when they reached Henrietta's tent there was a big sign that read SHOWS CANCELLED.

"Wow!" George whistled. "Henrietta really *can't* play without her lucky star."

The girls decided to spend the next hour playing their favorite carnival games—Hole in One, Cover the Dot, and Knock 'em Down. They didn't win any pandas, but they did win pretty plastic bracelets.

After slipping on the bracelets, Nancy and her friends met Hannah. She dropped them off at Orson's house.

"There he is," Bess whispered.

Nancy saw Orson sitting on his doorstep. He was spraying Frogzilla with a plastic water bottle.

"What are you doing?" Nancy asked.

"I'm spraying Frogzilla," Orson explained. "To keep him moist and limber."

"Blurrrp!" Frogzilla croaked.

"What are you doing here anyway?" Orson asked, not looking up.

"There's been trouble at the carnival," Nancy said. "Yesterday there were raw eggs in the potato sacks. And big black horseflies in the caterpillar."

"Today there was more trouble," George pointed out. "The Big Squirt—"

"Hel-lo?" Orson interrupted. "I wasn't at the carnival today."

Nancy looked at Bess and George. Should they believe Orson?

"Blurrrp!" Frogzilla croaked. Then he leaped off the doorstep.

"Frogzilla!" Orson cried. He stood up to grab his frog.

As Orson bent over Nancy saw something sticking out of his back pocket. It was his carnival passbook.

"Gotcha!" Nancy said, grabbing it.

"Hey!" Orson said. He spun around with Frogzilla in his hands.

Quickly, Nancy opened the passbook. It was stamped for Monday and Tuesday. But it wasn't stamped for Wednesday.

"See?" Orson said. "I wasn't at the carnival today. You've got the wrong man."

"But what about the horseflies in the caterpillar yesterday?" Bess asked. "Weren't those flies yours?"

"Yeah." Orson sighed. "But I didn't put them there on purpose."

"What do you mean?" Nancy asked.

"It was an accident," Orson said. "I was crawling through the caterpillar and the lid popped off the jar. Soon there were flies everywhere!"

"We know." Bess shuddered.

"The only way I could think of getting them back was with sugary stuff," Orson said. "So I bought a load of junk food."

Nancy looked at Bess and George. That explained all the candy.

"But what did you mean when you said, 'We'll show them'?" Nancy asked.

Orson rolled his eyes. "It means Frogzilla will be in the frog jumping contest *tomorrow*. We'll show them when we win."

Then Orson picked up Frogzilla. He grinned as he held him out to the girls.

"And maybe if you kiss him," Orson said, "he'll turn into a prince!"

"Blurrrrp!"

"Ewww!" Bess cried.

"Gross!" George exclaimed.

The girls ran from the Wong house. When they were two blocks away they turned to one another and giggled.

"That rules out Orson," George said.

"If it isn't Orson, and it isn't Cruncher," Bess asked. "Then who is it?"

Nancy stopped giggling. She had no more suspects and only a few hours left. But she was not going to give up.

"Let's get our bikes and ride back to the carnival," Nancy said. "There might be something we missed."

The girls got permission to ride their bikes to the carnival. They showed their passbooks at the gate and went in.

"Where do we start?" George asked.

"At Simon's," Bess said. "I could use another Little Boy Blueberry mini-pie."

"But you already had a mini-pie," Nancy said.

"That was almost two hours ago," Bess said.

Once again the girls lined up at Simon the Pieman's booth.

While Bess ordered a mini-pie, Nancy saw a colorful postcard pinned above the counter. It showed a lake and thick green trees.

"Who is that nice postcard from, Simon?" Nancy asked.

"Oh, that's from Nicky, Vicky, and Ricky," Simon said. "My kids are at sleepaway camp all summer."

"Camp?" Nancy repeated. "But—"

"Sure do miss them," Simon said. Then he called over Nancy's head. "Next!"

Nancy looked at Bess and George. Then the girls stepped away from the booth.

"If the triplets are in camp," Nancy said slowly. "Then who are the Three Little Pigs?"

8

Isabelle's Surprise

"T hose pigs *were* acting strange," George said. "All three of them."

When George held up three fingers Nancy saw her carnival tattoo. It hadn't washed off completely.

That's when it clicked. Jason, David, and Mike had had carnival tattoos on their hands. Maybe they *had* been at the carnival.

"Let's check out that pie booth," Nancy said. "There might be more in there than just yummy pies."

The girls ran back to the booth. While Simon served a customer, Nancy stood on the side of the counter and peeked in.

In the back of the booth was a pretty display of what Simon used to make his pies. On a table covered with a red tablecloth were a bowl of fruit, bottles of molasses, and a basket of white eggs.

"Eggs and molasses!" Nancy gasped.

Then Nancy noticed something else. The sign with the pie flavors was written with a black marker—the same kind of marker that had messed up Isabelle's cutout!

"Bess, George," Nancy said. "I think I know who's inside those costumes, and it's not the Three Little Pigs."

"Then who?" Bess asked.

"It's the Three Little Pests," Nancy said. "Jason, David, and Mike!"

Nancy, Bess, and George raced through the carnival. They found the Three Little Pigs on line at the slushy stand.

Very quietly the girls sneaked up behind the Three Little Pigs. They each grabbed a hood and yanked it off.

"Gotcha!" George shouted.

Jason, David, and Mike spun around. Their mouths dropped open.

"I thought you weren't going to the carnival this week," Nancy said. "And what are you doing dressed as the Three Little Pigs?"

"Don't bite our heads off!" Jason exclaimed.

"When Shirley wouldn't let us sing, Simon felt sorry for us," Mike said. "So he asked us to be the Three Little Pigs."

"And you showed your thanks by making trouble?" Nancy demanded.

"It wasn't us!" David insisted.

"No way!" Jason agreed.

Nancy decided to try to trick the boys into admitting what they'd done.

"Then what was Henrietta's lucky star doing behind the counter?" Nancy asked. She hadn't really seen the star there, though.

David turned to Mike. "I thought you put it in your backpack, dork!"

"I did!" Mike insisted. Then he turned red. "I mean . . . whoops."

"Busted." Jason sighed.

Nancy glared at the boys until they explained everything.

"We did most of the sneaky stuff before the carnival opened," Jason said. "Me and Mike put the eggs in the potato sacks while David helped Nina with the finish line."

"And Jason kept Trish busy while Mike and I slopped molasses on the squirt handles," David said.

"I was the one who snatched Henrietta's star," Mike said. "While Lou was eating a blueberry pie in his tent."

"It was easy sneaking around in these costumes," Jason said. "Everyone thought we were Nicky, Vicky, and Ricky. And who would suspect the Three Little Pigs?"

Nancy and her friends were practically speechless. How dare the boys spoil the carnival?

"Are you going to squeal on us?" Mike asked the girls.

"You'll be in less trouble if you apologize yourselves," Nancy said. "But if you don't tell, we will."

The boys grumbled as they grabbed their masks. Then they walked away.

"They're worried," Nancy said.

"How do you know?" Bess asked.

"They didn't buy slushies," Nancy pointed out happily.

"And you solved the case," George told Nancy. "Now Brenda won't write that article and give it to Isabelle tomorrow."

"And Isabelle will sing at the carnival!" Bess said, jumping up and down.

"Yippee!" Nancy cheered. "I'm going to call Brenda and tell her right now."

Nancy ran to a pay phone on the side of the school. There was a telephone book on a small shelf underneath.

Flipping through, Nancy found the Carltons' number. She dropped some coins into the telephone and pushed the numbers.

"Hello?" a woman's voice answered.

"Mrs. Carlton?" Nancy said. "This is Nancy Drew. Is Brenda home?"

"No, dear," Mrs. Carlton said. "Brenda went to deliver her paper."

Nancy gulped. "The *Carlton News*?"

"Yes," Mrs. Carlton said. "She said she was going to Isabelle Santoro's house. Somewhere on Chestnut Street, I believe."

Nancy stammered a quick goodbye and hung up. "Brenda wrote her article, and she's on her way to Isabelle's!" she cried. "We have to stop her!"

"Wait!" George said. She looked around. "Where's Bess?"

Nancy saw Bess running over. In her arms was a big stuffed panda.

"Look what I just won at the Big Squirt," Bess said. "For Isabelle!"

"Way to go!" Nancy said. She told Bess about Brenda as they ran out of the carnival. They jumped on their bikes and rode the five blocks to Chestnut Street.

"There's Brenda!" Nancy cried. "She's about to ring Isabelle's doorbell!"

The girls jumped off their bikes. Bess grabbed the panda from her basket.

"Brenda—stop!" Nancy called as they raced up the Santoros' path. "You said you'd deliver the paper tomorrow!"

Brenda looked at the paper in her hand and shrugged. "Early edition."

"That's not fair!" George shouted. "We just solved the case and—"

The door swung open.

"Hi," a voice said.

The girls whirled around. Nancy gasped. It was Isabelle Santoro!

"Oooh!" Isabelle said, smiling. "Is that for me?"

Brenda held out her paper. "Yes!"

"Not that," Isabelle said. "The panda. I love pandas!"

"We know," Bess said. She handed Isabelle the panda.

"Thanks!" Isabelle said. Then her dark eyes lit up. "Wait a minute. Are you all going to be at the carnival tomorrow?"

Nancy nodded.

"Because I could use girls like you for my act," Isabelle said.

"Your act?" Brenda cried. "You mean— like onstage? Really? Truly?"

"I thought you said she sings like a parrot," Bess whispered in Brenda's ear. "With crackers—"

Brenda gave Bess a hard nudge.

"Ouch!" Bess complained.

"When I sing 'It's My Secret,'" Isabelle said, "all you have to do is pretend you're whispering in one another's ears. It's a cinch!"

"We'll do it!" Brenda said. She shoved her newspaper behind her back.

"Cool!" Isabelle said. "Be at the carnival at one o'clock sharp. Shirley Vega will show you where to go."

Then Isabelle gave a little wave and went back into her house.

The girls stared at the door. Then they jumped up and down.

"Isabelle Santoro rocks!" Brenda cried.

"What happened to your article, Brenda?" George teased. "Aren't you going to deliver it to Isabelle?"

Nancy watched as Brenda tore her paper in half. "From now on, this will be *my* secret," she said.

"Good," Nancy said. "But don't forget. You still have to write about something nice at the carnival."

"I will," Brenda said. "How about this? 'Four third-graders become world-famous singing sensations!'"

Nancy, Bess, and George watched Brenda walk away. They turned to one another and gave high-fives.

Nancy felt on top of the world. Not only

had she solved another case—she and her friends were going to be onstage with Isabelle Santoro!

The next day Shirley whisked Nancy, Bess, George, and Brenda to a stage set up on the soccer field. Nancy wore her flowered pants and a yellow T-shirt. Bess was dressed in a pink polka-dotted sundress. Even George wore new blue pants and a crisp white T-shirt.

Brenda wore white pants and a gold shirt that read SUPERSTAR.

While Isabelle sang her song, the girls pretended to tell secrets.

"Everyone's here!" Bess whispered into Nancy's ear.

"I know!" Nancy whispered back.

Nancy glanced down from the stage. In the audience she saw her friends Rebecca, Katie, Molly, and Amara. Even Orson was there, waving Frogzilla and wearing a brand-new blue ribbon.

Not present were Jason, David, and Mike. After they confessed to Shirley they weren't allowed to return to the carnival.

"Isa-belle! Isa-belle! Isa-belle!" everyone shouted after the song.

When Isabelle climbed down from the stage Bess and George ran for her autograph. But Nancy had some of her own writing to do in her detective notebook.

Daddy was right again. There are always surprises at carnivals. And you never know what you'll find!

One thing I did find out—it doesn't pay to get even. In the end, nobody wins.

But maybe if I practice hard enough, next year I'll win the potato sack race. And maybe a brand-new panda!

Case closed.